Jimmy Tames Horses

Garry Gottfriedson

LONDON PUBLIC LIBRARY

Jimmy Tames Horses
© 2012 Garry Gottfriedson

Published by Kegedonce Press
Cape Croker First Nation, RR#5
Wiarton, ON Canada N0H 2T0
www.kegedonce.com

Editor: Paul Seesequasis
Cover & Story
Illustrations: Mary Longman
Book design: Cynthia Cake
for Wemakebooks.ca
Printed in Canada

All rights reserved. No part of this book
may be reproduced in any form or by
any electronic or mechanical means
including information storage and
retrieval systems, without permission in
writing from the Publisher. Member of
Access Copyright.

Kegedonce Press gratefully
acknowledges the generous
support of:
Ontario Arts Council
and **Canada Council for the Arts**
which last year invested
$20.1 million in writing
and publishing
throughout Canada.

ONTARIO ARTS COUNCIL
CONSEIL DES ARTS DE L'ONTARIO

The Canada Council for the Arts
Le Conseil des Arts du Canada

SALES AND DISTRIBUTION – Trade:
Literary Press Group of Canada
http://www.lpg.ca/

LitDistco:
For Customer Service/Orders
Tel 1-800-591-6250
Fax 1-800-591-6251
Email orders@litdistco.ca

100 Armstrong Avenue
Georgetown, ON L7G 5S4

DIRECT SALES:
www.kegedonce.com

Library and Archives Canada
Cataloguing in Publication

Gottfriedson, Garry, 1954-

    Jimmy tames horses / Garry
Gottfriedson ; illustrated

by Mary Longman.

ISBN 978-0-9868740-3-1

    1. Native children--Canada--
Juvenile fiction.

I. Longman, Mary, 1964- II. Title.

PS8563.O8388J54 2012   jC813'.6
C2012-901849-X

This book is dedicated
to my grandchildren:
Cobly, Rainbow, Paris
Keagan, Baby Girl,
Lance and Liam

WITHDRAWN

LONDON
PUBLIC LIBRARY

Jimmy did not grow up on the Reserve. He and his family had lived in Vancouver his whole life. But every summer, they stayed at the Reserve to visit relatives who lived on a ranch.

When they got there, Jimmy saw his cousins. They were wild and raging, riding and breaking horses. Jimmy was so excited he said that he would like to learn to ride horses too. But much to his horror, they teased and taunted him, saying, "You're just a city boy. You don't know anything about riding horses!" They ran away laughing.

Jimmy's feelings were hurt. He felt left out. Then he got an idea – a great idea. He was going to be a cowboy just like his cousins. "I'm gonna be the best horse-trainer in the entire world!" he said to himself.

Jimmy's Uncle Fred was the best horse-breaker in the province. Every day, Jimmy wandered over to the corrals to watch Uncle Fred break horses. His cousins never came around. They were out horseback riding or playing baseball, their favorite sport. They rarely invited Jimmy to join them. But Jimmy didn't mind, because nothing made him happier than watching Uncle Fred work with the horses.

One day, he asked Uncle Fred to teach him the secret of breaking horses. To his surprise, his uncle agreed. Jimmy was so excited, he could hardly sleep. The next morning he awoke at dawn and bounded toward the corrals. He helped his uncle pack flakes of hay and fill up the water buckets. He felt the wind in his hair and against his face. For the first time, Jimmy felt truly alive.

After the horses ate, he groomed them with the soft brush and fine finger curry comb - just the way Uncle Fred showed him. Then, he got the saddle blankets and saddles ready. After that, he ran to the barn for the bridles. He knew he had to learn to be comfortable with the horses. This is why Uncle Fred asked him to groom them.

Hour after hour Jimmy sat on the rail fence watching his uncle training horses in the round pen. He watched eagerly wondering when he would have his chance. The anticipation of breaking his first horse welled up inside of him. Every day, he imagined what it would be like to tame his first horse. Every night, he dreamed that he was the greatest horse trainer ever.

Uncle Fred saw Jimmy's passion grow. One day came he told Jimmy to choose a colt that he liked. Jimmy had not expected this. It was hard to decide. There were many handsome two year olds in the pens. He didn't know which one to pick. Then he saw a Palomino colt out of the corner of his eye. Jimmy knew right away that this horse was very special. This horse would change his whole life.

"I like the ivory coloured one over there," he told his uncle.

"Okay," said Uncle Fred, "then he's yours."

Jimmy was overjoyed. His own horse! He couldn't wait to get started. But he had to give his new pony a name. "What name should I give him?" he asked himself. "Oh, I know. I'll call him Bones."

He liked the name Bones because his new pony was the colour of bones.

Jimmy quickly got to work. He found a halter, saddle blanket and saddle that were just the right size for him. He rushed over to the corrals dragging them along the ground. Out of breath, he slung them onto the rail fence, just like he had seen Uncle Fred do.

Then he climbed over the fence and slowly walked over to Bones. So many feelings were rushing through him. He was trembling and breathless, a little scared and very happy all at once. Carefully, he put the halter around the horse's neck. Once he got it on, he could buckle it up.

He knew the steps for halter breaking from watching his uncle. Uncle Fred stood quietly inside the corral closely watching his nephew. Jimmy did everything right. It took days to halter break Bones. But soon, Bones trusted Jimmy and followed him everywhere.

Next, it was time to put the saddle blanket and saddle onto Bones.

At first, Bones didn't like it. He jumped and bucked and kicked high into the air. But after a while, he stopped and stood quietly. Jimmy was overcome with fear. Then he remembered what his uncle said, "never show the horse you are afraid of him."

Jimmy bravely walked over to where Bones was standing. He calmly grabbed onto the halter rope, and re-adjusted the saddle.

He walked his new colt round and round feeling the trust grow between them. Jimmy stroked Bones' face and silvery mane. When he looked into Bones' eyes, he could see the whole world. From then on Jimmy knew there was no reason ever to be afraid.

Uncle Fred watched proudly from over the fence rails.

Jimmy knew he had to put a bridle on Bones. He had already put the bridle on the corral gate where he could grab it easily. He led Bones towards the gate. Jimmy grabbed the bridle. He took his time putting the bridle on Bones. Bones was still a little nervous because all of this was new to him. But finally, he let Jimmy put the bridle on him.

Uncle Fred called out to Jimmy: "Jimmy, check the saddle to see if it is on safely. Make sure it's tight." It was a little loose, so Jimmy tightened it up.

"Now, slowly put your foot into the stirrup. Grab onto the saddle horn to brace yourself!" guided Uncle Fred.

Very slowly, Jimmy lifted himself into the stirrup. He didn't swing his leg all the way over the saddle. He had seen Uncle Fred do this many times, so he knew that he couldn't just jump on and ride right away.

Also, he wanted to make sure Bones wouldn't buck again. Bones shifted around a little bit, but he didn't buck. Jimmy did this again and again. After a while, Bones got used to the feel of Jimmy's body against his.

"Okay, now swing your leg over the saddle and just sit there," instructed Uncle Fred.

Jimmy did as he was told. Jimmy was a little frightened, but he didn't want to show it. Besides, Bones was cooperating. Jimmy sat frozen in the saddle for a few minutes. He didn't move. But Bones stood quietly. Jimmy felt better. He smiled to himself. Jimmy knew deep inside that he and Bones had formed an unbreakable bond.

"Okay, you and Bones are ready," Uncle Fred said. "Nudge him lightly in the ribs, and he will move for you."

Jimmy gently prodded Bones in the ribs to get him to walk. Bones took a few steps, then stopped. Jimmy nudged him again. This time Bones kept walking.

He rode Bones around in the pen for a long time. Jimmy steered Bones with the bridle reins just like the time he saw his dad drive a car.

Every day, Jimmy rode Bones around in the corral. Each time Jimmy rode Bones, the horse became tamer and tamer. Soon, Bones looked forward to Jimmy's arrival. Jimmy knew this, because when he walked to the pens to saddle up his ivory colt, Bones whinnied.

Before Jimmy knew it, the summer was coming to an end. It was almost time to return to Vancouver to go back to school. Jimmy spent every moment with Bones. Then one day, Uncle Fred said, "Jimmy, Bones is ready to be ridden in the mountains. Are you ready?"

Jimmy's heart was pounding with joy. He nodded, yes.

"Ok, let's go now," Uncle Fred told him.

Together, Jimmy and Uncle Fred rode through the village where his cousins were playing baseball. They stopped and stared. Jimmy was riding one of the two year olds! Jimmy smiled proudly at them as he rode past them towards the mountains.

Each summer after that, Jimmy broke many horses. He became a very famous horse breaker.

But he never forgot Bones, the horse that changed his life.

Author Bio

Garry Gottfriedson was born, raised and lives in Kamloops, BC. He is from the Secwepemc Nation. He is a self-employed rancher. Gottfriedson was also raised knowing Secwepemc songs and dances. Over the past few years, he has been teaching them at the Chief Atahm School as well as within his nation. He holds a Masters Degree in Education from the Simon Fraser University. In 1987, the Naropa Institute in Boulder, Colorado awarded the Gerald Red Elk Creative Writing Scholarship to Gottfriedson. There, he studied creative writing under Allen Ginsberg, Anne Waldman, Marianne Faithful and others. He has read from his work across Canada, United States, Europe, and Asia. His work has been anthologized and published nationally and internationally.

Books:

1 *Skin Like Mine*: Short-listed for the Canadian
  Authors Association Award
  for Poetry 2011 (Ronsdale Press: 2010)

2 *Whiskey Bullets*: Short-listed for the
  Anasi Award for Poetry 2007
  (Ronsdale Press: 2006)

3 *Painted Pony*: Children's book
  (Partners in Publishing: 2005)

4 *Glass Tepee*: Short-listed for
  First People's Publishing Award 2004
  (Thistledown Press: 2002)

5 *In Honor of Our Grandmothers*:
  Imprints of Cultural Survival
  (Theytus Books: 1994)

6 *100 Years of Contact*
  (Secwepemc Cultural
  Education Society: 1990)

Artist Bio

Mary Longman (Aski-Piyesiwiskwew) was born in Fort Qu'Appelle and is band member of Gordon First Nation. Dr. Longman is an interdisciplinary scholar, having taught Aboriginal Art History and Fine Art courses since 1989. She has also held senior academic positions as Dean at the White Mountain Academy of Arts in Elliot Lake, Ontario and Department Head of Fine Art at the Nicola Valley Institute of Technology in Merritt, BC. Currently she is an Associate Professor in Art & Art History at the University of Saskatchewan.

Mary Longman is also known nationally and internationally for her work as a professional artist specializing in the genres of sculpture, drawing and digital media. Her work has been shown at the Museum of Modern Art, NY, Smithsonian, NY, National Gallery of Canada, QC, Museum of Civilization, ONT, and the Vancouver Art Gallery, BC. Her education includes: Fine Art diploma (4 year) at the Emily Carr Institute of Art and Design, Vancouver a Masters degree in Fine Art at the Nova Scotia College of Art and Design, Halifax and a Ph.D at the University of Victoria, in Art Education, Victoria.